A Hundred Angels, Singing

by Dorothy Van Woerkom

The magic of a child's imagination at Christmas

> *Through the window's eye*
> *I watch and wonder—*
> *Was it cold, and*
> *Did the wind blow,*
> *Long ago when Jesus came?*

It's Christmas today, but this young girl's thoughts are far away. They weave in and out of the past and present. She sees beyond the wrapped gifts and tinseled tree. Her thoughts drift to Bethlehem and what happened ages ago.

A chilly night . . . a stranger at the door . . . a music box . . . through her eyes they reflect the first Christmas. All the little things around her lead her back to when Jesus was born.

Your children, too, will enjoy pretending along with this young girl. They'll join her as she lets her mind wander through Bethlehem to the manger, and to the Baby Jesus. The story helps your children see their own surroundings as a bridge to the night of Christ's birth.

The girl in the story comes closer to Jesus as she lets her imagination take her to Bethlehem on that night . . .

> *I pretend I'm standing with the*
> *Shepherds, and I hear*
> *A hundred angels,*
> *Singing!*

Recommended for 5- to 9-year-olds.

A Hundred Angels, Singing

A Hundred Angels, Singing

written by DOROTHY VAN WOERKOM

illustrated by Art Kirchhoff

Concordia Publishing House
St. Louis   London

Concordia Publishing House, St. Louis, Missouri
Copyright © 1976 by Concordia Publishing House

Manufactured in the United States of America

Library of Congress Cataloging in Publication Data

Van Woerkom, Dorothy.
    A hundred angels singing

    SUMMARY: A young girl reflects on the nativity
and compares it to her present day Christmas celebra-
tion.
    [1. Jesus Christ—Nativity—Fiction.]
I. Kirchhoff, Art. II. Title.
PZ7.V39Hu   [E]   76-12613
ISBN 0-570-03457-4

Remembering Joyce Marie Eddy
and Christmas long ago.

A chilly night: the cat wants in.
The rough wind speaks in whispers.
Trees make trembly shadows
On the ground.

Through the window's eye
I watch and wonder—
Was it cold, and
Did the wind blow,
Long ago when Jesus came?

A cloudless sky:
  One great white
  Star
  Glows brighter than the rest.

  How wise it looks.
  How old.
  It shines for me,
  As once it shone for Jesus
  On the night that He was born.

A music box:

It plays *O Little Town of Bethlehem*.
In the center there is Mary,
With the Baby in the manger.
Joseph and the shepherds stand nearby.

The little donkey nods its head.
The Wise Men march around the
Rim.
Oh, I love Christmas!

No snow in sight:
    There SHOULD be snow
    On Christmas Eve.
    "I hope it snows," I say to Mamma.

    "Never mind," she answers.
    "It will still be Christmas Eve
    Without it."
    So I pretend we live in Bethlehem
    And do not need the snow.

Two people walking in the street:
        See them hurry. They look cold!
        A light shines from a doorway.
        They climb the steps and go inside.

        They do not have to wait—
        As Mary did,
        And Joseph did—
        Or sleep on beds of prickly straw.

Hot chocolate in a big brown mug:
    I hold it in both hands.
    The steam floats up
    And warms my face.

    Warms it,
    Like the donkey's breath
    Warmed Jesus
    In the manger.

Mamma lights the tree:
    Red and green and yellow.
    Blue and white.
    She hums *O Holy Night*.

    I listen, and pretend
    I am a shepherd
    On the hillside.
    Waiting.
    Waiting.

Music on our doorstep:
  Girls and boys
  Have come with Christmas
  Songs.

  Daddy reaches high
  To put an angel on the treetop.
  I make believe
  This angel is a hundred angels,
  Singing.

Presents near the tree:
Fat and thin.
Square and squiggly.
I shake a long one, and it rattles.
The dog has chewed one open,
But I will not peek!

And I am glad
The Wise Men brought their gifts
To Jesus.

A knocking at our door:
    I am frightened.
    I am angry.
    "Go away!" I shout.

    A man has brought a package!
    I forgot that I was just
    Pretending.
    I thought the knock was one of Herod's
    Soldiers!

Bedtime: I don't want to go.
        I'm walking backwards up the stairs
        Still looking at the tree lights.
        Then
        A kiss for Mamma.
        "Say your prayers," she says.

        "But I don't want to pray," I tell her.
        "I just want to talk to Jesus."
        Mamma laughs and says, "That's praying!"

Daddy's footsteps:
    He brings the music box
    And sets it by my bed.
    "Now sleep," he says.
    "And dream of Christmas."

    I listen to the music as
    The donkey nods its head.
    The Wise Men march around the rim.
    I whisper, "Happy birthday, Jesus."

Two great big yawns:
> Excuse me, Jesus! I'm so sleepy.
> I blink—and all at once
> My night light is a star.

> The manger on the music box
> Grows larger.
> I pretend I'm standing with the
> Shepherds, and I hear
> A hundred angels,
> Singing!